LUNA

by Philemon Sturges

illustrated by Suling Wang

HOUGHTON MIFFLIN   BOSTON

Luna was a lovely caterpillar. She lived in a glass tank. Every morning, Saul brought Luna leaves to munch.

3

Saul talked to Luna every day. One day he said, "Luna, my Grandpa's sick. We're going to see him. I wish you could come."

"I wish I could too," Luna seemed to say.

So Saul asked his mom.

"I'm sorry, Saul. The tank's too big and heavy," she said.

Saul was sad and lonely at Grandpa's house. Grandpa was asleep most of the time. And Saul's mother was busy taking care of Grandpa.

Saul missed Luna. He wanted to tell her how lonely he was.

When they got home, Saul rushed in to see Luna. "Did you miss me?" he asked his caterpillar. Saul looked inside the tank.

Luna was gone. Saul looked all around his room. No Luna. "Mom!" Saul cried. "Luna is gone! Why did we have to go to Grandpa's?"

Mom hugged Saul. Then she said, "Grandpa couldn't take care of himself. Luna can. She's probably outside having a great time. But I'm sure she misses you."

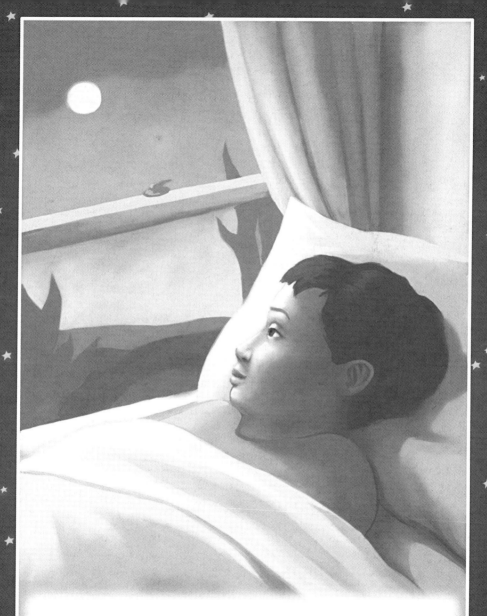

That night Saul watched the full moon rise and thought about Luna. Then he thought about Grandpa. And then he fell asleep.

When the moon came to the top of the sky, Saul woke up. A giant moth stood glowing in the moonlight.

"Climb on my back," she said. "Let's go for a ride."

They flew to the moon. Saul looked down. "The earth is beautiful!" he said.

"So it is," said the moth.

At breakfast Saul told his mother about the giant moth. Mom said, "You were dreaming. Moths don't carry people. And they can't fly to the moon!"

Then she smiled and said, "But sick people can get better! Grandpa just called. He took a long walk this morning."

That evening Saul found a rumpled something
in the tank. It looked like an old leaf. "I guess
that's what's left of Luna," he said to himself.

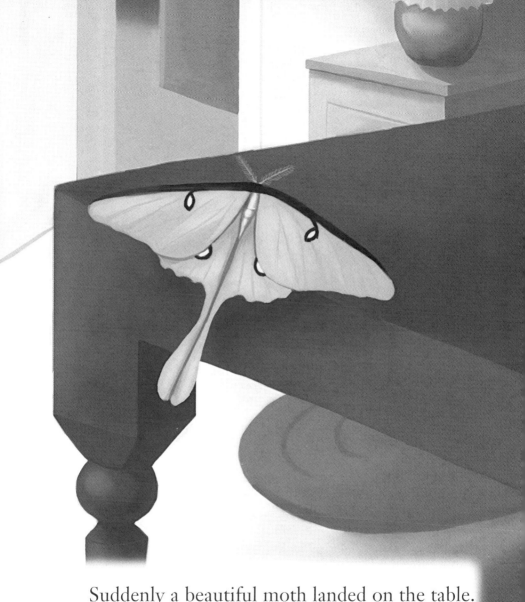

Suddenly a beautiful moth landed on the table.
It looked just like the moth in his dream, only
much smaller.

"I'm Luna," the moth seemed to say. "I've changed, that's all. But I'll always be your friend." Then Luna flew into the moonlit night.